This book belongs to

_____

Barbie ™
in
Wild Fire

Illustrations by Christian Musselman and Lily Glass
Cover illustration by Lawrence Mann

EGMONT

EGMONT

We bring stories to life

First published in Great Britain 2008
by Egmont UK Limited
239 Kensington High Street, London W8 6SA

BARBIE and associated trademarks and trade dress are owned by,
and used under licence from, Mattel, Inc.
© 2008 Mattel, Inc.

ISBN 978 1 4052 3844 1

1 3 5 7 9 10 8 6 4 2

Printed in Germany

Hello, my name is Willow and I am the Guardian of the Enchanted Forest.

This is a story about what happened when a baby dragon's sneeze nearly destroyed our forest . . .

It was early autumn in Willow's Enchanted Forest. The forest was aflame with colour. One by one the leaves had begun to fall – red, brown and gold – heaping up beneath the trees and along the tracks.

All day long, the animals gathered their winter stores and soon every nest, burrow and treehole was full of nuts, seeds and berries.

One evening, Willow and her friends sat around a campfire, telling stories and roasting chestnuts. But by the time the fire had turned to ashes, the animals were sound asleep in their beds.

Long after the nightingale's song had faded away, the animals woke again, one by one, to hear a strange snuffling and snorting coming from deep inside the forest.

"Listen – the trees are breathing!" squeaked the baby squirrels.

"Or the brown bear's got a sore head again," said the weasel.

"Help! The forest is haunted," cried Velvet, the little fawn. "We'd better wake Willow."

Oli told Willow of the strange noise in the forest.

"We mustn't worry," Willow soothed, "let's find out what it is. Come, Oli, come, Velvet!"

The rumbles and roars grew louder as they ventured deeper into the forest. Suddenly, a shower of sparks shot from the mouth of a cave. Willow crept closer, and came face-to-face with two frightened blue eyes peering out of the darkness.

Oli and Velvet turned and fled, but Willow was unafraid. At the entrance to the cave, she saw a little baby dragon, alone in the forest and very lost.

"Don't worry, little dragon," Willow laughed, "I'll take care of you!"

Slowly but surely, Willow coaxed the baby dragon out of the cave.

The dragon soon made friends with the forest animals and entertained them with a magical display of fiery tricks. He could huff and puff smoke rings, or vanish in a puff of smoke; he could fling yellow and orange flames high in the air or spit sparks like fireworks into the night sky.

Everybody cheered and applauded the dragon.

But suddenly, the baby dragon felt a tickle in his snout.

"Aaa . . . CHOOOO!" he sneezed, spluttering sparks in every direction.

The leaves and twigs were so dry and brittle that the sparks smouldered and caught fire. First the grass burned, then a bush, then a tree.

Soon the air was filled with the smell of smoke and the sound of crackling flames. As the wind fanned the flames, the whole forest was soon on fire.

The forest was in an uproar! The birds flew from their nests, animals panicked as they called their babies and everyone hurried towards the river as the flames spread. There was no time to take anything with them, not even their food stores!

Willow had to think quickly to save her forest friends. She called to Oli and Velvet, and the three friends ran to the river where the wise Rainbow Fish lived. "Our forest is disappearing in flames," Willow cried. "What can we do?"

"You must leave, of course," the Rainbow Fish warned. "Flee far away and wish for rain!"

Willow blew on her horn to call the Woodcutter Giant. "Please help us, we need to leave the forest and we need enough boats for us all."

The Giant was glad to help, and quickly he carved boats out of fallen trees. The animals clambered on board and sailed far away from the Enchanted Forest to safety.

Velvet found a place in one of the boats and called to Willow to join him as Oli fluttered nearby.

"But what about the dragon?" said Willow. "We must save him, too!"

Oli and Velvet began to protest. "He'll be far too much trouble!" grumbled Velvet.

"He might cause another fire!" Oli hooted.

Willow refused to leave the dragon behind. "He is only a baby," she reminded her friends. "The fire wasn't really his fault. It was an accident."

Willow brought her horn to her lips and with a long, clear note, summoned the little dragon to her side. The little dragon soon caught up with the fleet and was very pleased not to have been forgotten. Willow climbed aboard a boat, and the friends sailed away.

Willow and her friends watched from the riverbank with great sadness as the glowing forest burned to the ground. Finally, the flames died, and it was safe to return to the forest.

But it was not their Enchanted Forest anymore. Everything had been destroyed by the fire – even the precious food stores.

"We have nothing to eat, everything is spoilt!" sobbed the animals. "What will we do now?"

"Be patient," Willow soothed. "Let's wish for rain, as the Rainbow Fish told us. It's not too late."

Just then, Willow and her friends heard a beating of wings and looked up at the sky. A magnificent dragon flew overhead.

"Mama!" cried the baby dragon in delight, as his mother landed amongst the friends.

"My baby!" Mama Dragon sang. "I saw the flames from afar and suddenly I knew where to find you after you'd disappeared in the forest! You and your sneezes are always causing fires!" she laughed as she cuddled her child.

Mama Dragon was very pleased that Willow had kept her baby safe even though his sneeze had nearly destroyed the forest.

"I'd like to thank you for taking care of my baby. What would you like most of all in the world, dear Willow?" Mama Dragon asked the Guardian.

Willow thought for a moment and then she exclaimed, "Rain, please!"

So the dragon beat her wings, hard enough to bring thunder and lightning.

The rain began to fall.

Suddenly, little blades of grass sprang up here and there, and leaves uncurled on the trees and bushes.

The nuts, seeds and cones, blackened by the fire and trampled into the ground, split open and sprouted new shoots. The Enchanted Forest became lush and green again as if it were spring!

The baby dragon hopped onto his mother's back, and they flew away. Willow and her forest friends waved and called "Goodbye!" as the dragons vanished in two puffs of smoke on the horizon.

My *Barbie* Story Library

Barbie Story Library is THE definitive collection of stories about Barbie and her friends. Start your collection NOW and look out for even more titles to follow later!

ISBN: 978 1 4052 3105 3 • RRP: £2.99   ISBN: 978 1 4052 3106 0 • RRP: £2.99   ISBN: 978 1 4052 3107 7 • RRP: £2.99   ISBN: 978 1 4052 3108 4 • RRP: £2.99   ISBN: 978 1 4052 3109 1 • RRP: £2.99

A fantastic offer for Barbie fans!

In every Barbie Story Library book like this one, you will find a special token. Collect 5 tokens and we will send you a brilliant double-sided growing-up chart/poster for your wall!

Simply tape a £1 coin and a 50p coin in the spaces provided and fill out the form overleaf.

STICK £1 COIN HERE

STICK 50p COIN HERE

NOTE: Style of height chart may differ from that shown.

cut along the dotted line and return this whole page

To apply for this great offer, ask an adult to complete the details below and send this whole page with a £1 coin, a 50p coin and 5 tokens, to:
BARBIE OFFERS, PO BOX 715, HORSHAM RH12 5WG

☐ Please send me a Barbie™ growing-up chart/poster. I enclose 5 tokens plus £1.50 (price includes P&P).

Fan's name: .... Date of birth: ....

Address: ....

....

.... Postcode: ....

Email of parent / guardian: ....

Name of parent / guardian: ....

Signature of parent / guardian: ....

Please allow 28 days for delivery. Offer is only available while stocks last. We reserve the right to change the terms of this offer at any time and we offer a 14 day money back guarantee. This does not affect your statutory rights. Offers apply to UK only.

☐ We may occasionally wish to send you information about other Egmont children's books, including the next titles in the Barbie Story Library series. If you would rather we didn't, please tick this box.

Ref: BRB 001

cut along the dotted line and return this whole page